Road Works

Contents	Page

written by Rachel Walker

For many centuries, roads were rough paths and tracks used for horseback riding, walking, and horses pulling carriages or wagons. Cobblestones and bricks were used to form streets in towns and cities, where some still remain today.

With the invention of bicycles, and later cars, people wanted to travel further and faster. Better surfaces were needed to travel from place to place. More improvements had to be made as the numbers and types of vehicles grew.

In those early days, before modern machinery was available, building roads was extremely difficult. After the important planning stage to decide where the road needed to go, the next task - to clear the path - was often the hardest.

Big tree stumps, heavy rocks, smaller trees and plants all had to be removed to make way for the new road. Usually, this was done entirely by hand by a team of fit workmen using only simple tools like axes, saws, picks and shovels, or sometimes with ropes and the help of strong horses or oxen.

Once all of the obstacles were cleared away, the new roadway would be flattened and graded. The new road could be opened and used, but these rough dirt roads didn't last long before cracks, ruts and pot-holes formed. Dust was a problem, making it difficult to see hazards or other vehicles ahead.

Travel through muddy puddles and over bumps was extremely uncomfortable and slow, as damaged roads often caused delays or breakdowns. Road builders soon learned to add drainage ditches at the sides of the roadways, so that rainwater could run off the surface.

To build a more permanent road that would last longer and be safer for people using the road, a top layer of stone was added. The more layers of big stones and smaller pieces of gravel that were put on the roads, the better they became, and the longer they lasted without needing repairs. Gravel roads are still used today in country areas without much traffic.

Modern day roads are formed with the help of heavy machinery and strong materials. Manpower and horsepower have been replaced by modern earthmoving equipment and vehicles such as:

- Diggers
- Graders
- Rollers
- Bulldozers
- Dump trucks

Nowadays, road builders are not stopped by obstacles like rocks and cliffs. They use dynamite to blast through mountains and hillsides, building tunnels to take the roads through places that were once blocked. Deep gullies and swift rivers can be easily crossed on roads built on bridges and causeways. Flyovers can take one road over another.

The only thing that hasn't changed is the most important first step in the process: **planning**.

Planners need to understand the impact that the new road will make on the environment, and do whatever can be done to limit damage where roads are essential. Instead of building a road through a valley and ruining the natural habitat, an answer could be: to build a causeway or bridge over the top to reduce the impact and preserve the habitat for its creatures.

Construction stages:

- First the foundation of a new road must be built higher than the land on each side to drain away rainwater.
- A layer of broken rock is covered with layers of crushed rock and fine gravel.
- Heavy rollers are driven back and forth to pack these layers down, making them strong and firm.
- Modern roads are sealed with a mixture like asphalt or concrete to seal in the dust and keep the water out, making a smooth, hard driving surface for vehicles.

sealing

Thousands of tons of rainwater fall on roadways each year, so they must be shaped as they are being built - higher in the middle and lower at the sides - to help drain off the water. But there is also water underground, so engineers must do a lot of drainage work under the earth, too. This work is to make sure that the water trapped below the road can escape, and won't cause wash-outs, cracks or potholes.

grader

Driving:
Surveyors check that every road is as level as possible, but drivers need to manage slopes, hills and corners. Engineers make sure that each road is shaped to help vehicles to travel around corners easily and safely. Warning signs are put up, speed limits are set, and lines are painted on the roadway to help drivers and passengers get from place to place safely.

After a long time, traffic and weather wear out the road surface. Rough patches, bumps and pot-holes need skilful repair work immediately to prevent accidents. New sealing is done whenever necessary to replace worn-out surfaces, keeping roads smooth and strong for drivers, passengers, and heavy loads of goods.

Wherever road works are happening, you can expect to see signs that warn drivers to slow down and take extra care. There will be people and machines moving backward and forward as they work to build, repair, or even improve the road: e.g. by straightening or widening.

Roads can lead over hills, around corners, through forests, and across rivers on bridges. They can cross over mountain ranges or even take you through mountains and cliffs using tunnels. Wherever the road takes you, remember to take care on the roads for safe and happy travels!

END
ROAD WORK

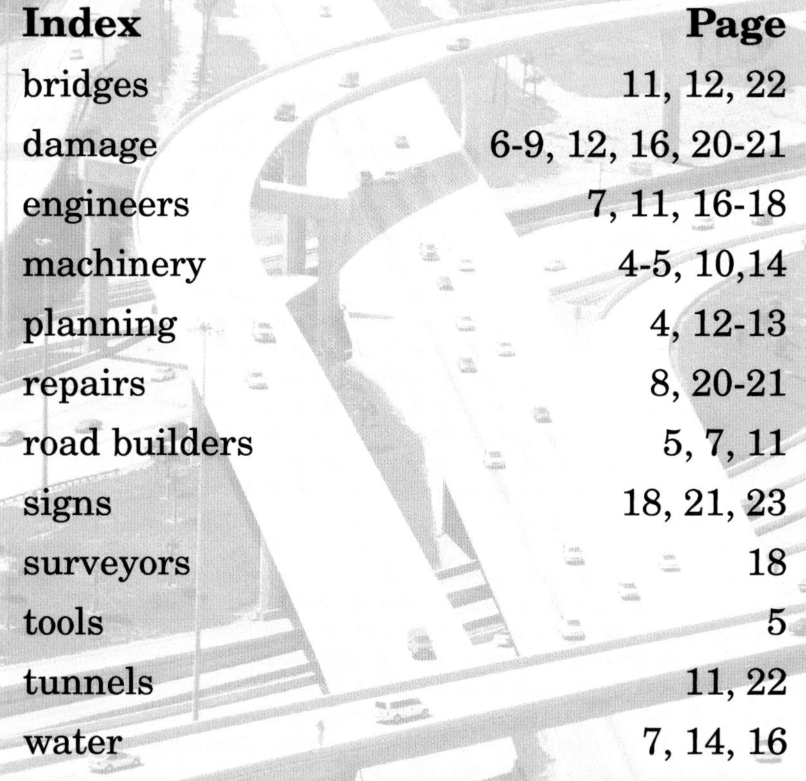

Index	Page
bridges	11, 12, 22
damage	6-9, 12, 16, 20-21
engineers	7, 11, 16-18
machinery	4-5, 10,14
planning	4, 12-13
repairs	8, 20-21
road builders	5, 7, 11
signs	18, 21, 23
surveyors	18
tools	5
tunnels	11, 22
water	7, 14, 16